English Fairy Tales

A Children's Classic

ENGLISH
FAIRY TALES

Twelve Classic Tales

*

SELECTED AND ILLUSTRATED BY

EDWARD ARDIZZONE

FROM THE COLLECTION OF

JOSEPH JACOBS

ANDRE DEUTSCH

FIRST PUBLISHED IN HARDCOVER 1980 BY
ANDRE DEUTSCH LIMITED
105-106 GREAT RUSSELL STREET, LONDON WC1B 3LJ

ILLUSTRATIONS COPYRIGHT © 1980
THE ESTATE OF EDWARD ARDIZZONE
ALL RIGHTS RESERVED

SECOND HARDBACK IMPRESSION JANUARY 1987
THIRD HARDBACK IMPRESSION MAY 1987
FIRST PAPERBACK EDITION 1987

ISBN HARDBACK EDITION 0 233 98129 2
ISBN PAPERBACK EDITION 0 233 98127 6

PRINTED IN GREAT BRITAIN BY
EBENEZER BAYLIS AND SON LIMITED, WORCESTER

WHEN EDWARD ARDIZZONE died in November 1979 he was at work on the illustrations for a selection of twenty-five of the English Folk Tales collected and edited by the folklorist, Joseph Jacobs. He had illustrated eleven of the stories, which are presented in this book.

The illustration for the twelfth story, *The Children in the Wood*, first appeared in an edition of this poem published by The Bodley Head in 1972.

CONTENTS

*

Jack the Giant-Killer

*

WHEN GOOD KING ARTHUR REIGNED, there lived near the Land's End of England, in the county of Cornwall, a farmer who had one only son called Jack. He was brisk and of ready, lively wit, so that nobody or nothing could worst him.

In those days the Mount of Cornwall was kept by a huge giant named Cormoran. He was eighteen feet in height, and about three yards round the waist, of a fierce and grim countenance, the terror of all the neighbouring towns and villages. He lived in a cave in the midst of the Mount, and whenever he wanted food he would wade over to the mainland, where he would furnish himself with whatever came in his way. Everybody at his approach ran out of their houses, while he seized on their cattle, making nothing of carrying half a dozen oxen on his back at a time; and as for their sheep and hogs, he would tie them round his waist like a bunch of tallow-dips. He had done this for many years, so that all Cornwall was in despair.

One day Jack happened to be at the town-hall when the magistrates were sitting in council about the giant. He asked: 'What reward will be given to the man who kills Cormoran?' 'The giant's treasure,' they said, 'will be the reward.' Quoth Jack: 'Then let me undertake it.'

So he got a horn, shovel, and pickaxe, and went over to the Mount in the beginning of a dark winter's evening, when he fell to work, and before morning had dug a pit twenty-two feet deep, and nearly as broad, covering it over with long sticks and straw. Then he strewed a little mould over it, so that it appeared like plain ground. Jack then placed himself on the opposite side of the pit, farthest from the giant's lodging, and, just at the break of day, he put the horn to his mouth, and blew, Tantivy, Tantivy. This noise roused the giant, who rushed from his cave, crying: 'You incorrigible villain, are you come here to disturb my rest? You shall pay dearly for this. Satisfaction I will have, and this it shall be, I will take you whole and broil you for breakfast.' He had no sooner uttered this, than he tumbled into the pit, and made the very foundations of the Mount to shake. 'Oh, Giant,' quoth Jack, 'where are you now? Oh, faith, you are gotten now into Lob's Pound, where I will surely plague you for your threatening words; what do you think now of broiling me for your breakfast? Will no other diet serve you but poor Jack?' Then having tantalised the giant for a while, he gave him a most weighty knock with his pickaxe on the very crown of his head, and killed him on the spot.

Jack then filled up the pit with earth, and went to search the cave, which he found contained much treasure. When the magistrates heard of this they made a declaration he should henceforth be termed

JACK THE GIANT-KILLER,

and presented him with a sword and a belt, on which were written these words embroidered in letters of gold:

'Here's the right valiant Cornish man,
Who slew the giant Cormoran.'

The news of Jack's victory soon spread over all the West of England, so that another giant, named Blunderbore, hearing of it, vowed to be revenged on Jack, if ever he should light on him. This giant was the lord of an enchanted castle situated in the midst of a lonesome wood. Now Jack, about four months afterwards, walking near this wood in his journey to Wales, being weary, seated himself near a pleasant fountain and fell fast asleep. While he was sleeping the giant, coming there for water, discovered him, and knew him to be the far-famed Jack the Giant-Killer by the lines written on the belt. Without ado, he took Jack on his shoulders and carried him towards his castle. Now, as they passed through a thicket, the rustling of the boughs awakened Jack, who was strangely surprised to find himself in the clutches of the giant. His terror was only begun, for, on entering the castle, he saw the ground strewed with human bones, and the giant told him his own would ere long be among them. After this the giant locked poor Jack in an immense chamber, leaving him there while he went to fetch another giant, his brother, living in the same wood, who might share in the meal on Jack.

After waiting some time Jack, on going to the window, beheld afar off the two giants coming towards the castle. 'Now,' quoth Jack to himself, 'my death or my deliverance is at hand.' Now, there were strong cords in a corner of the room in which Jack was, and two of these he took, and made a strong noose at the end; and while the giants were unlocking the iron gate of the castle he threw the ropes over each of their heads. Then he drew the other ends across a beam, and pulled with all his might, so that he throttled them. Then, when he saw they were black in the face, he slid down the rope, and drawing his sword, slew them both. Then, taking the giant's keys, and unlocking the rooms, he found three fair ladies tied by the hair of their heads, almost starved to death. 'Sweet ladies,' quoth Jack, 'I have destroyed this monster and his brutish brother, and obtained your liberties.' This said he presented them with the keys, and so proceeded on his journey to Wales.

Jack made the best of his way by travelling as fast as he could, but lost his road, and was benighted, and could find no habitation until, coming into a narrow valley, he found a large house, and in order to get shelter took courage to knock at the gate. But what was his surprise when there came forth a monstrous giant with two heads; yet he did not appear so fiery as the others were, for he was a Welsh giant, and what he did was by private and secret malice under the false show of friendship. Jack, having told his condition to the giant, was shown into a bedroom, where, in the dead of night, he heard his host in another apartment muttering these words:

'Though here you lodge with me this night,
You shall not see the morning light:
My club shall dash your brains outright!'

'Say'st thou so,' quoth Jack; 'that is like one of your Welsh tricks, yet I hope to be cunning enough for you.' Then, getting out of bed, he laid a billet in the bed in his stead, and hid himself in a corner of the room. At the dead time of the night in came the Welsh giant, who struck several heavy blows on the bed with his club, thinking he had broken every bone in Jack's skin. The next morning Jack, laughing in his sleeve, gave him hearty thanks for his night's lodging, 'How have you rested?' quoth the giant; 'did you not feel anything in the night?' 'No,' quoth Jack, 'nothing but a rat, which gave me two or three slaps with her tail.' With that, greatly wondering, the giant led Jack to breakfast, bringing him a bowl containing four gallons of hasty pudding. Being loth to let the giant think it too much for him, Jack put a large leather bag under his loose coat, in such a way that he could convey the pudding into it without its being perceived. Then, telling the giant he would show him a trick, taking a knife, Jack ripped open the bag, and out came all the hasty pudding. Whereupon, saying, 'Odds splutters her nails, hur can do that trick hurself', the monster took the knife, and ripping open his belly, fell down dead.

Now, it happened in these days that King Arthur's only son asked his father to give him a large sum of money, in order that he might go and seek his fortune in the principality of Wales, where lived a beautiful lady possessed with seven evil spirits. The king did his best to persuade his son from it, but in vain; so at last gave way and the prince set out with two horses, one loaded with money, the other for himself to ride upon. Now, after several days' travel, he came to a market-town in Wales, where he beheld a vast crowd of people gathered together. The prince asked the reason of it, and was told that they had arrested a corpse for several large sums of money which the deceased owed when he died. The prince replied that it was a pity creditors should be so cruel, and said: 'Go bury your dead, and let his creditors come to my lodging, and there their debts shall be paid.' They came, in such great numbers that before night he had only twopence left for himself.

Now Jack the Giant-Killer, coming that way, was so taken with the generosity of the prince that he desired to be his servant. This being agreed upon, the next morning they set forward on their journey together, when, as they were riding out of the town, an old woman called after the prince, saying, 'He has owed me twopence these seven years; pray pay me as well as the rest.' Putting his hand into his pocket, the prince gave the woman all he had left, so that after their day's food, which cost what small store Jack had by him, they were without a penny between them.

When the sun got low, the king's son said: 'Jack, since we have no money, where can we lodge this night?'

But Jack replied: 'Master, we'll do well enough, for I have an uncle lives within two miles of this place; he is a huge and monstrous giant with three heads; he'll fight five hundred men in armour, and make them to fly before him.'

'Alas!' quoth the prince, 'what shall we do there? He'll

certainly chop us up at a mouthful. Nay, we are scarce enough to fill one of his hollow teeth!'

'It is no matter for that,' quoth Jack: 'I myself will go before and prepare the way for you; therefore stop here and wait till I return.' Jack then rode away at full speed, and coming to the gate of the castle, he knocked so loud that he made the neighbouring hills resound. The giant roared out at this like thunder: 'Who's there?'

Jack answered: 'None but your poor cousin Jack.'

Quoth he: 'What news with my poor cousin Jack?'

He replied: 'Dear uncle, heavy news, God wot!'

'Prithee,' quoth the giant, 'what heavy news can come to me? I am a giant with three heads, and besides thou knowest I can fight five hundred men in armour, and make them fly like chaff before the wind.'

'Oh, but,' quoth Jack, 'here's the king's son a-coming with a thousand men in armour to kill you and destroy all that you have!'

'Oh, cousin Jack,' said the giant, 'this is heavy news indeed! I will immediately run and hide myself, and thou shalt lock, bolt, and bar me in, and keep the keys until the prince is gone.' Having secured the giant, Jack fetched his master, when they made themselves heartily merry whilst the poor giant lay trembling in a vault under the ground.

Early in the morning Jack furnished his master with a fresh supply of gold and silver, and then sent him three miles forward on his journey, at which time the prince was pretty well out of the smell of the giant. Jack then returned, and let the giant out of the vault, who asked what he should give him for keeping the castle from destruction. 'Why,' quoth Jack, 'I want nothing but the old coat and cap, together with the old rusty sword and slippers which are at your bed's head.' Quoth the giant: 'You know not what you ask; they are the most precious things I have. The coat will keep you invisible, the cap will tell you all you want to know, the sword cuts asunder whatever you strike, and the shoes are of extraordinary swiftness. But you have been very serviceable to me therefore take them with all my heart.' Jack thanked his uncle, and then went off with them. He soon overtook his master and they quickly arrived at the house of the lady the prince sought, who, finding the prince to be a suitor, prepared a splendid banquet for him. After the repast was concluded, she told him she had a task for him. She wiped his mouth with a handkerchief, saying: 'You must show me that handkerchief tomorrow morning, or else you will lose your head.' With that she put it in her bosom. The prince went to bed in great sorrow, but Jack's cap of knowledge informed him how it was to be obtained. In the middle of the night she called upon her familiar spirit to carry her to Lucifer. But Jack put on his coat of darkness and his shoes of swiftness, and was there as soon as she was. When she entered the place of the demon, she gave the handkerchief to him, and he laid it upon a shelf, whence Jack took it and brought it to his master, who showed it to the lady next day, and so saved his life. On that day, she gave the prince a kiss and told him he must show her the lips tomorrow morning that she kissed last night, or lose his head.

'Ah!' he replied, 'if you kiss none but mine, I will.'

'That is neither here nor there,' said she; 'if you do not, death's your portion!'

At midnight she went as before, and was angry with the demon for letting the handkerchief go. 'But now,' quoth she, 'I will be too hard for the king's son, for I will kiss thee, and he is to show me thy lips.' Which she did, and Jack, when she was not standing by, cut off Lucifer's head and brought it under his invisible coat to his master, who the next morning pulled it out by the horns before the lady. This broke the enchantment and the evil spirit left her, and she appeared in all her beauty. They were married the next morning, and soon after went to the Court of King Arthur, where Jack for his many great exploits, was made one of the Knights of the Round Table.

Jack soon went searching for giants again, but he had not ridden far, when he saw a cave, near the entrance of which he beheld a giant sitting upon a block of timber, with a knotted iron club by his side. His goggle eyes were like flames of fire, his countenance grim and ugly, and his cheeks like a couple of large flitches of bacon, while the bristles of his beard resembled rods of iron wire, and the locks that hung down upon his brawny shoulders were like curled snakes or hissing adders. Jack alighted from his horse, and, putting on the coat of darkness, went up close to the giant, and said softly: 'Oh! are you there? It will not be long before I take you fast by the beard.' The giant all this while could not see him, on account of his invisible coat, so that Jack, coming up close to the monster, struck a blow with his sword at his head, but, missing his aim, he cut off the nose instead. At this, the giant roared like claps of thunder, and began to lay about him with his iron club like one stark mad. But Jack, running behind, drove his sword up to the hilt in the giant's back, so that he fell down dead. This done, Jack cut off the giant's head, and sent it, with his brother's also, to King Arthur, by a waggoner he hired for that purpose.

Jack now resolved to enter the giant's cave in search of his treasure, and, passing along through a great many windings and turnings, he came at length to a large room paved with freestone, at the upper end of which was a boiling caldron, and on the right hand a large table, at which the giant used to dine. Then he came to a window, barred with iron, through which he looked and beheld a vast number of miserable captives, who, seeing him, cried out: 'Alas! young man, art thou come to be one amongst us in this miserable den?'

'Ay,' quoth Jack, 'but pray tell me what is the meaning of your captivity?'

'We are kept here,' said one, 'till such time as the giants have a wish to feast, and then the fattest among us is slaughtered! And many are the times they have dined upon murdered men!'

'Say you so,' quoth Jack, and straightway unlocked the gate and let them free, who all rejoiced like condemned men at sight of a pardon. Then searching the giant's coffers, he shared the gold and silver equally amongst them and took them to a neighbouring castle, where they all feasted and made merry over their deliverance.

But in the midst of all this mirth a messenger brought news that one Thunderdell, a giant with two heads, having heard of the death of his kinsmen, had come from the northern dales to be revenged on Jack, and was within a mile of the castle, the country people flying before him like chaff. But Jack was not a bit daunted, and said: 'Let him come! I have a tool to pick his teeth; and you, ladies and gentlemen, walk out into the garden, and you shall witness this giant Thunderdell's death and destruction.'

The castle was situated in the midst of a small island surrounded by a moat thirty feet deep and twenty feet wide, over which lay a drawbridge. So Jack employed men to cut through this bridge on both sides, nearly to the middle; and then, dressing himself in his invisible coat, he marched against the giant with his sword of sharpness. Although the giant could not see Jack, he smelt his approach, and cried out in these words:

> 'Fee, fi, fo, fum!
> I smell the blood of an Englishman!
> Be he alive or be he dead,
> I'll grind his bones to make me bread!'

'Say'st thou so,' said Jack; 'then thou art a monstrous miller indeed.'

The giant cried out again: 'Art thou that villain who killed my kinsmen? Then I will tear thee with my teeth, suck thy blood, and grind thy bones to powder.'

'You'll have to catch me first,' quoth Jack, and throwing off his invisible coat, so that the giant might see him, and putting on his shoes of swiftness, he ran from the giant, who followed like a walking castle, so that the very foundations of the earth seemed to shake at every step. Jack led him a long dance, in order that the gentlemen and ladies might see; and at last to end the matter, ran lightly over the drawbridge, the giant, in full speed, pursuing him with his club. Then, coming to the middle of the bridge, the giant's great weight broke it down, and he tumbled headlong into the water, where he rolled and wallowed like a whale. Jack, standing by the moat, laughed at him all the while; but though the giant foamed to hear him scoff, and plunged from place to place in the moat, yet he could not get out to be revenged. Jack at length got a cart rope and cast it over the two heads of the giant and drew him ashore by a team of horses, and then cut off both his heads with his sword of sharpness, and sent them to King Arthur.

After some time spent in mirth and pastime, Jack, taking leave of the knights and ladies, set out for new adventures. Through many woods he passed, and came at length to the foot of a high mountain. Here, late at night, he found a lonesome house, and knocked at the door, which was opened by an aged man with a head as white as snow. 'Father,' said Jack, 'can you lodge a benighted traveller that has lost his way?' 'Yes,' said the old man; 'you are right welcome to my poor cottage.' Whereupon Jack entered, and down they sat together, and the old man began to speak as follows: 'Son, I see by your belt you are the great conqueror of giants, and behold, my son, on the top of this mountain is an enchanted castle; this is kept by a giant named Galligantua, and he, by the help of an old conjurer, betrays many knights and ladies into his castle, where by magic art they are transformed into sundry shapes and forms. But

above all, I grieve for a duke's daughter, whom they fetched from her father's garden, carrying her through the air in a burning chariot drawn by fiery dragons, when they secured her within the castle, and transformed her into a white hind. And though many knights have tried to break the enchantment, and work her deliverance, yet no one could accomplish it, on account of two dreadful griffins which are placed at the castle gate and which destroy everyone who comes near. But you, my son, may pass by them undiscovered, where on the gates of the castle you will find engraved in large letters how the spell may be broken.' Jack gave the old man his hand, and promised that in the morning he would venture his life to free the lady.

In the morning Jack arose and put on his invisible coat and magic cap and shoes, and prepared himself for the fray. Now when he had reached the top of the mountain he soon discovered the two fiery griffins, but passed them without fear, because of his invisible coat. When he had got beyond them, he found upon the gates of the castle a golden trumpet hung by a silver chain, under which these lines were engraved:

'Whoever shall this trumpet blow,
Shall soon the giant overthrow,
And break the black enchantment straight;
So all shall be in happy state.'

Jack had no sooner read this but he blew the trumpet, at which the castle trembled to its vast foundations, and the giant and conjurer were in horrid confusion, biting their thumbs and tearing their hair, knowing their wicked reign was at an end. Then the giant stooping to take up his club, Jack at one blow cut off his head; whereupon the conjurer, mounting up into the air, was carried away in a whirlwind. Then the enchantment was broken, and all the lords and ladies who had so long been transformed into birds and beasts returned to their proper shapes, and the castle vanished away in a cloud of smoke. This being done, the head of Galligantua was likewise, in the usual manner, conveyed to the Court of King Arthur, where, the very next day, Jack followed, with the knights and ladies who had been delivered. Whereupon, as a reward for his good services, the king prevailed upon the duke to bestow his daughter in marriage on honest Jack. So married they were, and the whole kingdom was filled with joy at the wedding. Furthermore, the king bestowed on Jack a noble castle, with a very beautiful estate thereto belonging, where he and his lady lived in great joy and happiness all the rest of their days.

Henny-penny

*

ONE DAY Henny-penny was picking up corn in the cornyard when – whack! – something hit her upon the head. 'Goodness gracious me!' said Henny-penny; 'the sky's a-going to fall; I must go and tell the king.'

So she went along and she went along and she went along till she met Cocky-locky. 'Where are you going, Henny-penny?' says Cocky-locky. 'Oh! I'm going to tell the king the sky's a-falling,' says Henny-penny. 'May I come with you?' says Cocky-locky. 'Certainly,' says Henny-penny. So Henny-penny and Cocky-locky went to tell the king the sky was falling.

They went along, and they went along, and they went along, till they met Ducky-daddles. 'Where are you going to, Henny-penny and Cocky-locky?' says Ducky-daddles. 'Oh! we're going to tell the king the sky's a-falling,' said Henny-penny and Cocky-locky. 'May I come with you?' says Ducky-daddles. 'Certainly,' said Henny-penny and Cocky-locky. So Henny-penny, Cocky-locky, and Ducky-daddles went to tell the king the sky was a-falling.

So they went along, and they went along, and they went along, till they met Goosey-poosey. 'Where are you going to, Henny-penny, Cocky-locky, and Ducky-daddles?' said Goosey-poosey. 'Oh! we're going to tell the king the sky's a-falling,' said Henny-penny and Cocky-locky and Ducky-daddles. 'May I come with you?' said Goosey-poosey. 'Certainly,' said Henny-penny, Cocky-locky, and Ducky-daddles. So Henny-penny, Cocky-locky, Ducky-daddles, and Goosey-poosey went to tell the king the sky was a-falling.

So they went along, and they went along, and they went along, till they met Turkey-lurkey. 'Where are you going, Henny-penny, Cocky-locky, Ducky-daddles, and Goosey-poosey?' says Turkey-lurkey. 'Oh! we're going to tell the king the sky's a-falling,' said Henny-penny, Cocky-locky, Ducky-daddles, and Goosey-poosey. 'May I come with you, Henny-penny, Cocky-locky, Ducky-daddles, and Goosey-poosey?' said Turkey-lurkey. 'Oh, certainly, Turkey-lurkey,' said Henny-penny, Cocky-locky, Ducky-daddles, and Goosey-poosey. So Henny-penny, Cocky-locky, Ducky-daddles, Goosey-poosey, and Turkey-lurkey all went to tell the king the sky was a-falling.

So they went along, and they went along, and they went along, till they met Foxy-woxy, and Foxy-woxy said to Henny-penny, Cocky-locky, Ducky-daddles, Goosey-poosey, and Turkey-lurkey: 'Where are you going, Henny-penny, Cocky-locky, Ducky-daddles, Goosey-poosey, and Turkey-lurkey?' And Henny-penny, Cocky-locky, Ducky-daddles, Goosey-poosey, and Turkey-lurkey said to Foxy-woxy: 'We're going to tell the king the sky's a-falling.' 'Oh! but this is not the way to the king, Henny-penny, Cocky-locky, Ducky-daddles, Goosey-poosey, and Turkey-lurkey,' says Foxy-woxy; 'I know the proper way; shall I show it you?' 'Oh, certainly, Foxy-woxy,' said Henny-penny, Cocky-locky, Ducky-daddles, Goosey-poosey, and Turkey-lurkey. So Henny-penny, Cocky-locky, Ducky-daddles, Goosey-poosey, Turkey-lurkey, and Foxy-woxy all went to tell the king the sky was a-falling. So they went along, and they went along, and they went along, till they came to a narrow and dark hole. Now this was the door of Foxy-woxy's cave. But Foxy-woxy said to Henny-penny, Cocky-locky, Ducky-daddles, Goosey-poosey, and Turkey-lurkey: 'This is the short way to the king's palace: you'll soon get there if you follow me. I will go first and you come after, Henny-penny, Cocky-locky, Ducky-daddles, Goosey-poosey, and Turkey-lurkey.' 'Why, of course, certainly, without doubt, why not?' said Henny-penny, Cocky-locky, Ducky-daddles, Goosey-poosey, and Turkey-lurkey.

So Foxy-woxy went into his cave, and he didn't go very far, but turned round to wait for Henny-penny, Cocky-locky, Ducky-daddles, Goosey-poosey, and Turkey-lurkey. So at last at first Turkey-lurkey went through the dark hole into the cave. He hadn't got far when 'Hrumph', Foxy-woxy snapped off Turkey-lurkey's head and threw his body over his left shoulder. Then

Goosey-poosey went in, and 'Hrumph', off went her head and Goosey-poosey was thrown beside Turkey-lurkey. Then Ducky-daddles waddled down, and 'Hrumph', snapped Foxy-woxy, and Ducky-daddles's head was off and Ducky-daddles was thrown alongside Turkey-lurkey and Goosey-poosey. Then Cocky-locky strutted down into the cave, and he hadn't gone far when 'Snap, Hrumph!' went Foxy-woxy, and Cocky-locky was thrown alongside of Turkey-lurkey, Goosey-poosey, and Ducky-daddles.

But Foxy-woxy had made two bites at Cocky-locky, and when the first snap only hurt Cocky-locky, but didn't kill him, he called out to Henny-penny. But she turned tail and off she ran home, so she never told the king the sky was a-falling.

Tom Tit Tot

*

ONCE UPON A TIME there was a woman, and she baked five pies. And when they came out of the oven, they were that over-baked the crusts were too hard to eat. So she says to her daughter:

'Darter,' says she, 'put you them there pies on the shelf, and leave 'em there a little, and they'll come again.' – She meant, you know, the crust would get soft.

But the girl, she says to herself: 'Well, if they'll come again, I'll eat 'em now.' And she set to work and ate 'em all, first and last.

Well, come supper-time the woman said: 'Go you, and get one o' them there pies. I dare say they've come again now.'

The girl went and she looked, and there was nothing but the dishes. So back she came and says she: 'Noo, they ain't come again.'

'Not one of 'em?' says the mother.

'Not one of 'em,' says she.

'Well, come again, or not come again,' said the woman, 'I'll have one for supper.'

'But you can't, if they ain't come,' said the girl.

'But I can,' says she. 'Go you, and bring the best of 'em.'

'Best or worst,' says the girl, 'I've ate 'em all, and you can't have one till that's come again.'

Well, the woman she was done, and she took her spinning to the door to spin, and as she span she sang:

'My darter ha' ate five, five pies today.
My darter ha' ate five, five pies today.'

The king was coming down the street, and he heard her sing, but what she sang he couldn't hear, so he stopped and said:

[25]

'What was that you were singing, my good woman?'

The woman was ashamed to let him hear what her daughter had been doing, so she sang, instead of that:

'My darter ha' spun five, five skeins today.
My darter ha' spun five, five skeins today.'

'Stars o' mine!' said the king, 'I never heard tell of anyone that could do that.'

Then he said: 'Look you here, I want a wife, and I'll marry your daughter. But look you here,' says he, 'eleven months out of the year she shall have all she likes to eat, and all the gowns she likes to get, and all the company she likes to keep; but the last month of the year, she'll have to spin five skeins every day, and if she don't I shall kill her.'

'All right,' says the woman; for she thought what a grand marriage that was. And as for the five skeins, when the time came, there'd be plenty of ways of getting out of it, and likeliest, he'd have forgotten all about it.

Well, so they were married. And for eleven months the girl had all she liked to eat, and all the gowns she liked to get, and all the company she liked to keep.

But when the time was getting over, she began to think about the skeins and to wonder if he had 'em in mind. But not one word did he say about 'em, and she thought he'd wholly forgotten 'em.

However, the last day of the last month he takes her to a room she'd never set eyes on before. There was nothing in it but a spinning-wheel and a stool. And says he: 'Now, my dear, here you'll be shut in tomorrow with some victuals and some flax, and if you haven't spun five skeins by the night, your head'll go off.'

And away he went about his business.

Well, she was that frightened, she'd always been such a gatless girl, that she didn't so much as know how to spin, and what was she to do tomorrow with no one to come nigh her to help her? She sat down on a stool in the kitchen, and law! how she did cry!

However, all of a sudden she heard a sort of a knocking low down on the door. She upped and oped it, and what should she see but a small little black thing with a long tail. That looked up at her right curious, and that said:

'What are you a-crying for?'

'What's that to you?' says she.

'Never you mind,' that said, 'but tell me what you're a-crying for.'

'That won't do me no good if I do,' says she.

'You don't know that,' that said, and twirled that's tail round.

'Well,' says she, 'that won't do no harm, if that don't do no good,' and she upped and told about the pies, and the skeins, and everything.

'This is what I'll do,' says the little black thing, 'I'll come to your window every morning and take the flax and bring it spun at night.'

'What's your pay?' says she.

That looked out of the corner of that's eyes, and that said:

'I'll give you three guesses every night to guess my name, and if you haven't guessed it before the month's up you shall be mine.'

Well, she thought, she'd be sure to guess that's name before the month was up. 'All right,' says she, 'I agree.'

'All right,' that says, and law! how that twirled that's tail.

Well, the next day, her husband took her into the room, and there was the flax and the day's food.

'Now, there's the flax,' says he, 'and if that ain't spun up this night, off goes your head.' And then he went out and locked the door.

He'd hardly gone, when there was a knocking against the window.

She upped and she oped it, and there sure enough was the little old thing sitting on the ledge.

'Where's the flax?' says he.

'Here it be,' says she. And she gave it to him.

Well, come the evening a knocking came again to the window.

[27]

She upped and she oped it, and there was the little old thing with five skeins of flax on his arm.

'Here it be,' says he, and he gave it to her.

'Now, what's my name?' says he.

'What, is that Bill?' says she.

'Noo, that ain't,' says he, and he twirled his tail.

'Is that Ned?' says she.

'Noo, that ain't,' says he, and he twirled his tail.

'Well, is that Mark?' says she.

'Noo, that ain't,' says he, and he twirled his tail harder, and away he flew.

Well, when her husband came in, there were the five skeins ready for him. 'I see I shan't have to kill you tonight, my dear,' says he; 'you'll have your food and your flax in the morning,' says he, and away he goes.

Well, every day the flax and the food were brought, and every day that there little black impet used to come mornings and evenings. And all the day the girl sate trying to think of names to say to it when it came at night. But she never hit on the right one. And as it got towards the end of the month, the impet began to look so maliceful, and that twirled that's tail faster and faster each time she gave a guess.

At last it came to the last day but one. The impet came at night along with the five skeins, and that said:

'What, ain't you got my name yet?'

'Is that Nicodemus?' says she.

'Noo, 't ain't,' that says.

'Is that Sammle?' says she.

'Noo, 't ain't,' that says.

'A-well, is that Methusalem?' says she.

'Noo, 't ain't that neither,' that says.

Then that looks at her with that's eyes like a coal of fire, and that says: 'Woman, there's only tomorrow night, and then you'll be mine!' And away it flew.

Well, she felt that horrid. However. she heard the king coming along the passage. In he came, and when he sees the five skeins, he says, says he:

'Well, my dear,' says he. 'I don't see but what you'll have your skeins ready tomorrow night as well, and as I reckon I shan't have to kill you, I'll have supper in here tonight.' So they brought supper, and another stool for him, and down the two sate.

Well, he hadn't eaten but a mouthful or so, when he stops and begins to laugh.

'What is it?' says she.

'A-why,' says he, 'I was out a-hunting today, and I got away to a place in the wood I'd never seen before. And there was an old chalk-pit. And I heard a kind of a sort of humming. So I got off my hobby, and I went right quiet to the pit, and I looked down. Well, what should there be but the funniest little black thing you ever set eyes on. And what was that doing, but that had a little spinning-wheel, and that was spinning wonderful fast, and twirling that's tail. And as that span that sang:

> 'Nimmy nimmy not
> My name's Tom Tit Tot.'

Well, when the girl heard this, she felt as if she could have jumped out of her skin for joy, but she didn't say a word.

Next day that there little thing looked so maliceful when he came for the flax. And when night came she heard that knocking against the window panes. She oped the window, and that come right in on the ledge. That was grinning from ear to ear, and Oo! that's tail was twirling round so fast.

'What's my name?' that says, as that gave her the skeins.

'Is that Solomon?' she says, pretending to be afraid.

'Noo, 't ain't,' that says, and that came further into the room.

'Well, is that Zebedee?' says she again.

'Noo, 't ain't,' says the impet. And then that laughed and twirled that's tail till you couldn't hardly see it.

'Take time, woman,' that says; 'next guess, and you're mine.' And that stretched out that's black hands at her.

Well, she backed a step or two, and she looked at it, and then she laughed out, and says she, pointing her finger at it:

'Nimmy nimmy not
Your name's Tom Tit Tot.'

Well, when that heard her, that gave an awful shriek and away
that flew into the dark, and she never saw it any more.

The Children in the Wood

*

Now PONDER WELL, you parents dear,
  These words which I shall write;
A doleful story you shall hear,
  In time brought forth to light.
A gentleman of good account,
  In Norfolk dwelt of late,
Who did in honour far surmount
  Most men of his estate.

Sore sick he was and like to die,
  No help his life could save;
His wife by him as sick did lie,
  And both possest one grave.
No love between these two was lost,
  Each was to other kind;
In love they lived, in love they died,
  And left two babes behind.

The one a fine and pretty boy
  Not passing three years old,
The other a girl more young than he,
  And framed in beauty's mould.
The father left his little son,
  As plainly did appear,
When he to perfect age should come,
  Three hundred pounds a year;

And to his little daughter Jane
　　Five hundred pounds in gold,
To be paid down on marriage-day,
　　Which might not be controlled.
But if the children chanced to die
　　Ere they to age should come,
Their uncle should possess their wealth;
　　For so the will did run.

'Now, brother,' said the dying man,
　　'Look to my children dear;
Be good unto my boy and girl,
　　No friends else have they here;
To God and you I recommend
　　My children dear this day;
But little while be sure we have
　　Within this world to stay.

'You must be father and mother both,
　　And uncle, all in one;
God knows what will become of them
　　When I am dead and gone.'
With that bespake their mother dear:
　　'O brother kind,' quoth she,
'You are the man must bring our babes
　　To wealth or misery.

'And if you keep them carefully,
　　Then God will you reward;
But if you otherwise should deal,
　　God will your deeds regard.'
With lips as cold as any stone,
　　They kissed their children small:
'God bless you both, my children dear!'
　　With that the tears did fall.

These speeches then their brother spake
  To this sick couple there:
'The keeping of your little ones,
  Sweet sister, do not fear;
God never prosper me nor mine,
  Nor aught else that I have,
If I do wrong your children dear
  When you are laid in grave!'

The parents being dead and gone,
  The children home he takes,
And brings them straight unto his house
  Where much of them he makes.
He had not kept these pretty babes
  A twelvemonth and a day,
But, for their wealth, he did devise
  To take them both away.

He bargained with two ruffians strong,
  Which were of furious mood,
That they should take these children young,
  And slay them in a wood.
He told his wife an artful tale
  He would the children send
To be brought up in London town
  With one that was his friend.

Away then went those pretty babes,
  Rejoicing at that tide,
Rejoicing with a merry mind
  They should on cock-horse ride,
They prate and prattle pleasantly,
  As they ride on the way,
To those that should their butchers be
  And work their lives' decay:

So that the pretty speech they had
  Made Murder's heart relent;
And they that undertook the deed
  Full sore now did repent.
Yet one of them, more hard of heart,
  Did vow to do his charge,
Because the wretch that hired him
  Had paid him very large.

The other won't agree thereto,
  So there they fall to strife;
With one another they did fight
  About the children's life;
And he that was of mildest mood
  Did slay the other there,
Within an unfrequented wood;
  The babes did quake for fear!

He took the children by the hand,
  Tears standing in their eye,
And bade them straightway follow him,
  And look they did not cry;
And two long miles he led them on,
  While they for food complain:
'Stay here,' quoth he, 'I'll bring you bread,
  When I come back again.'

These pretty babes, with hand in hand,
  Went wandering up and down;
But never more could see the man
  Approaching from the town.
Their pretty lips with blackberries
  Were all besmeared and dyed;
And when they saw the darksome night,
  They sat them down and cried.

Thus wandered these poor innocents,
  Till death did end their grief;
In one another's arms they died,
  As wanting due relief:
No burial this pretty pair
  From any man receives,
Till Robin Redbreast piously
  Did cover them with leaves.

And now the heavy wrath of God
  Upon their uncle fell;
Yea, fearful fiends did haunt his house,
  His conscience felt an hell.
His barns were fired, his goods consumed,
  His lands were barren made,
His cattle died within the field,
  And nothing with him stayed.

And in a voyage to Portugal
  Two of his sons did die;
And to conclude, himself was brought
  To want and misery.
He pawned and mortgaged all his land
  Ere seven years came about.
And now at last this wicked act
  Did by this means come out.

The fellow that did take in hand
　　These children for to kill,
Was for a robbery judged to die.
　　Such was God's blessed will:
Who did confess the very truth,
　　As here hath been displayed:
The uncle having died in jail,
　　Where he for debt was laid.

You that executors be made,
　　And overseers eke,
Of children that be fatherless,
　　And infants mild and meek,
Take you example by this thing,
　　And yield to each his right,
Lest God with suchlike misery
　　Your wicked minds requite.

Jack and the Beanstalk

*

THERE WAS ONCE UPON A TIME a poor widow who had an only son named Jack, and a cow named Milky-white. And all they had to live on was the milk the cow gave every morning, which they carried to the market and sold. But one morning Milky-white gave no milk, and they didn't know what to do.

'What shall we do, what shall we do?' said the widow, wringing her hands.

'Cheer up, mother, I'll go and get work somewhere,' said Jack.

'We've tried that before, and nobody would take you,' said his mother; 'we must sell Milky-white and with the money start shop, or something.'

'All right, mother,' says Jack; 'it's market-day today, and I'll soon sell Milky-white, and then we'll see what we can do.'

So he took the cow's halter in his hand, and off he started.

He hadn't gone far when he met a funny-looking old man, who said to him: 'Good morning, Jack.'

'Good morning to you,' said Jack, and wondered how he knew his name.

'Well, Jack, and where are you off to?' said the man.

'I'm going to market to sell our cow here.'

'Oh, you look the proper sort of chap to sell cows,' said the man; 'I wonder if you know how many beans make five.'

'Two in each hand and one in your mouth,' says Jack, as sharp as a needle.

'Right you are,' says the man, 'and here they are, the very beans themselves,' he went on, pulling out of his pocket a number of strange-looking beans. 'As you are so sharp,' says he, 'I don't mind doing a swop with you – your cow for these beans.'

'Go along,' says Jack; 'wouldn't you like it?'

'Ah! you don't know what these beans are,' said the man; 'if you plant them overnight, by morning they grow right up to the sky.'

'Really?' said Jack; 'you don't say so.'

'Yes, that is so, and if it doesn't turn out to be true you can have your cow back.'

'Right,' says Jack, and hands him over Milky-white's halter and pockets the beans.

Back goes Jack home, and as he hadn't gone very far it wasn't dusk by the time he got to his door.

'Back already, Jack?' said his mother; 'I see you haven't got Milky-white, so you've sold her. How much did you get for her?'

'You'll never guess, mother,' says Jack.

'No, you don't say so. Good boy! Five pounds, ten, fifteen, no, it can't be twenty.'

'I told you you couldn't guess. What do you say to these beans; they're magical, plant them overnight and – '

'What!' says Jack's mother, 'have you been such a fool, such a dolt, such an idiot, as to give away my Milky-white, the best milker in the parish, and prime beef to boot, for a set of paltry beans? Take that! Take that! Take that! And as for your precious beans here they go out of the window. And now off with you to bed. Not a sup shall you drink, and not a bit shall you swallow this very night.'

So Jack went upstairs to his little room in the attic, and sad and sorry he was, to be sure, as much for his mother's sake, as for the loss of his supper.

At last he dropped off to sleep.

When he woke up, the room looked so funny. The sun was shining into part of it, and yet all the rest was quite dark and shady. So Jack jumped up and dressed himself and went to the window. And what do you think he saw? Why, the beans his mother had thrown out of the window into the garden had sprung up into a big beanstalk which went up and up and up till it reached the sky. So the man spoke truth after all.

The beanstalk grew up quite close past Jack's window, so all he had to do was to open it and give a jump on to the bean-stalk which ran up just like a big ladder. So Jack climbed, and he climbed and he climbed and he climbed and he climbed and he climbed and he climbed till at last he reached the sky. And when he got there he found a long broad road going as straight as a dart. So he walked along and he walked along and he walked along till he came to a great big tall house, and on the doorstep there was a great big tall woman.

'Good morning, mum,' says Jack, quite polite-like. 'Could you be so kind as to give me some breakfast?' For he hadn't had anything to eat, you know, the night before and was as hungry as a hunter.

'It's breakfast you want, is it?' says the great big tall woman, 'it's breakfast you'll be if you don't move off from here. My man is an ogre and there's nothing he likes better than boys broiled on toast. You'd better be moving on or he'll soon be coming.'

'Oh! please, mum, do give me something to eat, mum. I've had nothing to eat since yesterday morning, really and truly, mum,' says Jack. 'I may as well be broiled as die of hunger.'

Well, the ogre's wife was not half so bad after all. So she took Jack into the kitchen, and gave him a hunk of bread and cheese and a jug of milk. But Jack hadn't half finished these when thump! thump! thump! the whole house began to tremble with the noise of someone coming.

'Goodness gracious me! It's my old man,' said the ogre's wife, 'what on earth shall I do? Come along quick and jump in here.' And she bundled Jack into the oven just as the ogre came in.

He was a big one, to be sure. At his belt he had three calves strung up by the heels, and he unhooked them and threw them down on the table and said: 'Here, wife, broil me a couple of these for breakfast. Ah! what's this I smell?

'Fee-fi-fo-fum,
I smell the blood of an Englishman,
Be he alive, or be he dead
I'll have his bones to grind my bread.'

'Nonsense, dear,' said his wife, 'you're dreaming. Or perhaps you smell the scraps of that little boy you liked so much for yesterday's dinner. Here, you go and have a wash and tidy up, and by the time you come back your breakfast'll be ready for you.'

So off the ogre went, and Jack was just going to jump out of the oven and run away when the woman told him not. 'Wait till he's asleep,' says she; 'he always has a doze after breakfast.'

Well, the ogre had his breakfast, and after that he goes to a big chest and takes out of it a couple of bags of gold, and down he sits and counts till at last his head began to nod and he began to snore till the whole house shook again.

Then Jack crept out on tiptoe from his oven, and as he was passing the ogre he took one of the bags of gold under his arm, and off he pelters till he came to the beanstalk, and then he threw down the bag of gold, which, of course, fell into his mother's garden, and then he climbed down and climbed down till at last he got home and told his mother and showed her the gold and said: 'Well, mother, wasn't I right about the beans? They are really magical, you see.'

[41]

So they lived on the bag of gold for some time, but at last they came to the end of it, and Jack made up his mind to try his luck once more at the top of the beanstalk. So one fine morning he rose up early, and got on to the beanstalk, and he climbed and he climbed and he climbed and he climbed and he climbed and he climbed till at last he came out on to the road again and up to the great big tall house he had been to before. There, sure enough, was the great big tall woman a-standing on the doorstep.

'Good morning, mum,' says Jack, as bold as brass, 'could you be so good as to give me something to eat?'

'Go away, my boy,' said the big tall woman, 'or else my man will eat you up for breakfast. But aren't you the youngster who came here once before? Do you know, that very day my man missed one of his bags of gold.'

'That's strange, mum,' said Jack, 'I dare say I could tell you something about that, but I'm so hungry I can't speak till I've had something to eat.'

Well, the big tall woman was so curious that she took him in and gave him something to eat. But he had scarcely begun munching it as slowly as he could when thump! thump! they heard the giant's footstep, and his wife hid Jack away in the oven.

All happened as it did before. In came the ogre as he did before, said: 'Fe-fi-fo-fum', and had his breakfast of three broiled oxen. Then he said: 'Wife, bring me the hen that lays the golden eggs.' So she brought it, and the ogre said: 'Lay,' and it laid an egg all of gold. And then the ogre began to nod his head, and to snore till the house shook.

Then Jack crept out of the oven on tiptoe and caught hold of the golden hen, and was off before you could say 'Jack Robinson'. But this time the hen gave a cackle which woke the ogre, and just as Jack got out of the house he heard him calling: 'Wife, wife, what have you done with my golden hen?'

And the wife said: 'Why, my dear?'

But that was all Jack heard, for he rushed off to the beanstalk and climbed down like a house on fire. And when he got home he showed his mother the wonderful hen, and said 'Lay' to it; and it laid a golden egg every time he said 'Lay'.

Well, Jack was not content, and it wasn't very long before he determined to have another try at his luck up there at the top of the beanstalk. So one fine morning, he rose up early, and got on to the beanstalk, and he climbed and he climbed and he climbed and he climbed till he got to the top. But this time he knew better than to go straight to the ogre's house. And when he got near it, he waited behind a bush till he saw the ogre's wife come out with a pail to get some water, and then he crept into the house and got into the copper. He hadn't been there long when he heard thump! thump! thump! as before, and in came the ogre and his wife.

'Fee-fi-fo-fum, I smell the blood of an Englishman,' cried out the ogre. 'I smell him, wife, I smell him.'

'Do you, my dearie?' says the ogre's wife. 'Then, if it's that little rogue that stole your gold and the hen that laid the golden eggs he's sure to have got into the oven.' And they both rushed over to the oven. But Jack wasn't there, luckily, and the ogre's wife said: 'There you are again with your fee-fi-fo-fum. Why, of course, it's the boy you caught last night that I've just broiled for your breakfast. How forgetful I am, and how careless you are not to know the difference between live and dead after all these years.'

So the ogre sat down to the breakfast and ate it, but every now and then he would mutter: 'Well, I could have sworn – ' and he'd get up and search the larder and the cupboards and everything, only, luckily, he didn't think of the copper.

After breakfast was over, the ogre called out: 'Wife, wife, bring me my golden harp.' So she brought it and put it on the table before him. Then he said: 'Sing!' and the golden harp sang most beautifully. And it went on singing till the ogre fell asleep, and commenced to snore like thunder.

Then Jack lifted up the copper-lid very quietly and got down like a mouse and crept on hands and knees till he came to the table, when up he crawled, caught hold of the golden harp and dashed with it towards the door. But the harp called out quite loud: 'Master! Master!' and the ogre woke up just in time to see Jack running off with his harp.

Jack ran as fast as he could, and the ogre came rushing after, and would soon have caught him only Jack had a start and dodged him a bit and knew where he was going. When he got to the beanstalk the ogre was not more than twenty yards away when suddenly he saw Jack disappear like, and when he came to the end of the road he saw Jack underneath climbing down for dear life. Well, the ogre didn't like trusting himself to such a ladder, and stood and waited, so Jack got another start. But just then the harp cried out: 'Master! Master!' and the ogre swung himself down on to the beanstalk, which shook with his weight. Down climbs Jack, and after him climbed the ogre. By this time Jack had climbed down and climbed down and climbed down till he was very nearly home. So he called out: 'Mother! Mother! bring me an axe, bring me an axe.' And his mother came rushing out with the axe in her hand, but when she came to the beanstalk she stood stock still with fright, for there she saw the ogre with his legs just through the clouds.

But Jack jumped down and got hold of the axe and gave a chop at the beanstalk which cut it half in two. The ogre felt the beanstalk shake and quiver, so he stopped to see what was the matter. Then Jack gave another chop with the axe, and the beanstalk was cut in two and began to topple over. Then the ogre fell down and broke his crown, and the beanstalk came toppling after.

Then Jack showed his mother his golden harp, and what with showing that and selling the golden eggs, Jack and his mother became very rich, and he married a great princess, and they lived happy ever after.

Cap o' Rushes

*

WELL, there was once a very rich gentleman, and he had three daughters, and he thought he'd see how fond they were of him. So he says to the first, 'How much do you love me, my dear?'

'Why,' says she, 'as I love my life.'

'That's good,' says he.

So he says to the second, 'How much do *you* love me, my dear?'

'Why,' says she, 'better nor all the world.'

'That's good,' says he.

So he says to the third, 'How much do *you* love me, my dear?'

'Why, I love you as fresh meat loves salt,' says she.

Well, but he was angry. 'You don't love me at all,' says he, 'and in my house you stay no more.' So he drove her out there and then, and shut the door in her face.

Well, she went away on and on till she came to a fen, and there she gathered a lot of rushes and made them into a kind of a sort of a cloak with a hood, to cover her from head to foot, and to hide her fine clothes. And then she went on and on till she came to a great house.

'Do you want a maid?' says she.

'No, we don't,' said they.

'I haven't nowhere to go,' says she; 'and I ask no wages, and do any sort of work,' says she.

'Well,' said they, 'if you like to wash the pots and scrape the saucepans you may stay,' said they.

So she stayed there and washed the pots and scraped the saucepans and did all the dirty work. And because she gave no name they called her 'Cap o' Rushes'.

Well, one day there was to be a great dance a little way off, and the servants were allowed to go and look on at the grand people. Cap o' Rushes said she was too tired to go, so she stayed at home.

But when they were gone, she offed with her cap o' rushes, and cleaned herself, and went to the dance. And no one there was so finely dressed as she.

Well, who should be there but her master's son, and what should he do but fall in love with her the minute he set eyes on her. He wouldn't dance with anyone else.

But before the dance was done, Cap o' Rushes slipt off, and away she went home. And when the other maids came back, she was pretending to be asleep with her cap o' rushes on.

Well, next morning they said to her, 'You did miss a sight, Cap o' Rushes!'

'What was that?' says she.

'Why, the beautifullest lady you ever see, dressed right gay and ga'. The young master, he never took his eyes off her.'

'Well, I should have liked to have seen her,' says Cap o' Rushes.

'Well, there's to be another dance this evening, and perhaps she'll be there.'

But, come the evening, Cap o' Rushes said she was too tired to go with them. Howsoever, when they were gone, she offed with her cap o' rushes and cleaned herself, and away she went to the dance.

The master's son had been reckoning on seeing her, and he danced with no one else, and never took his eyes off her. But, before the dance was over, she slipt off, and home she went, and when the maids came back she pretended to be asleep with her cap o' rushes on.

Next day they said to her again, 'Well, Cap o' Rushes, you should ha' been there to see the lady. There she was again, gay and ga', and the young master he never took his eyes off her.'

'Well, there,' says she, 'I should ha' liked to ha' seen her.'

'Well,' says they, 'there's a dance again this evening, and you must go with us, for she's sure to be there.'

Well, come this evening, Cap o' Rushes said she was too tired to go, and do what they would she stayed at home. But when they were gone, she offed her cap o' rushes and cleaned herself, and away she went to the dance.

The master's son was rarely glad when he saw her. He danced with none but her and never took his eyes off her. When she wouldn't tell him her name, nor where she came from, he gave her a ring and told her if he didn't see her again he should die.

Well, before the dance was over, off she slipped, and home she went, and when the maids came home she was pretending to be asleep with her cap o' rushes on.

Well, next day they says to her, 'There, Cap o' Rushes, you didn't come last night, and now you won't see the lady, for there's no more dances.'

'Well, I should have rarely liked to have seen her,' says she.

The master's son tried every way to find out where the lady was gone, but go where he might, and ask whom he might he never heard anything about her. And he got worse and worse for the love of her till he had to keep his bed.

'Make some gruel for the young master,' they said to the cook. 'He's dying for the love of the lady.' The cook set about making it when Cap o' Rushes came in.

'What are you a-doing of?' says she.

'I'm going to make some gruel for the young master,' says the cook, 'for he's dying for love of the lady.'

'Let me make it,' says Cap o' Rushes.

Well, the cook wouldn't at first, but at last she said yes, and Cap o' Rushes made the gruel. And when she had made it, she slipped the ring into it on the sly before the cook took it upstairs.

The young man he drank it and then he saw the ring at the bottom.

'Send for the cook,' says he.

So up she comes.

'Who made this gruel here?' says he.

'I did,' says the cook, for she was frightened.

And he looked at her.

[49]

'No, you didn't,' says he. 'Say who did it, and you shan't be harmed.'

'Well, then, 'twas Cap o' Rushes,' says she.

'Send Cap o' Rushes here,' says he.

So Cap o' Rushes came.

'Did you make my gruel?' says he.

'Yes, I did,' says she.

'Where did you get this ring?' says he.

'From him that gave it me,' says she.

'Who are you, then?' says the young man.

'I'll show you,' says she. And she offed with her cap o' rushes, and there she was in her beautiful clothes.

Well, the master's son he got well very soon, and they were to be married in a little time. It was to be a very grand wedding, and everyone was asked far and near. And Cap o' Rushes's father was asked. But she never told anybody who she was.

But before the wedding, she went to the cook, and says she:

'I want you to dress every dish without a mite o' salt.'

'That'll be rare nasty,' says the cook.

'That doesn't signify,' says she.

'Very well,' says the cook.

Well, the wedding day came, and they were married. And after they were married, all the company sat down to the dinner. When they began to eat the meat, it was so tasteless they couldn't eat it, But Cap o' Rushes's father tried first one dish and then another, and then he burst out crying.

'What is the matter?' said the master's son to him.

'Oh!' says he, 'I had a daughter. And I asked her how much she loved me. And she said "As much as fresh meat loves salt." And I turned her from my door, for I thought she didn't love me. And now I see she loved me best of all. And she may be dead for ought I know.'

'No, father, here she is!' said Cap o' Rushes. And she goes up to him and puts her arms round him.

And so they were all happy ever after.

Mr Fox

*

LADY MARY was young, and Lady Mary was fair. She had two brothers, and more lovers than she could count. But of them all, the bravest and most gallant was a Mr Fox, whom she met when she was down at her father's country house. No one knew who Mr Fox was; but he was certainly brave, and surely rich, and of all her lovers Lady Mary cared for him alone. At last it was agreed upon between them that they should be married. Lady Mary asked Mr Fox where they should live, and he described to her his castle, and where it was; but, strange to say, did not ask her or her brothers to come and see it.

So one day, near the wedding day, when her brothers were out, and Mr Fox was away for a day or two on business, as he said, Lady Mary set out for Mr Fox's castle. And after many searchings, she came at last to it, and a fine strong house it was, with high walls and a deep moat. And when she came up to the gateway she saw written on it:

Be bold, be bold.

But as the gate was open, she went through it, and found no one there. So she went up to the doorway, and over it she found written:

Be bold, be bold, but not too bold.

Still she went on, till she came into the hall, and went up the broad stairs till she came to a door in the gallery, over which was written:

Be bold, be bold, but not too bold,
Lest that your heart's blood should run cold.

But Lady Mary was a brave one, she was, and she opened the door, and what do you think she saw? Why, bodies and skeletons of beautiful young ladies all stained with blood. So Lady Mary thought it was high time to get out of that horrid place, and she closed the door, went through the gallery, and was just going down the stairs, and out of the hall, when who should she see through the window but Mr Fox dragging a beautiful young lady along from the gateway to the door. Lady Mary rushed downstairs, and hid herself behind a cask, just in time, as Mr Fox came in with the poor young lady, who seemed to have fainted. Just as he got near Lady Mary, Mr Fox saw a diamond ring glittering on the finger of the young lady he was dragging, and he tried to pull it off. But it was tightly fixed, and would not come off, so Mr Fox cursed and swore, and drew his sword, raised it, and brought it down upon the hand of the poor lady. The sword cut off the hand, which jumped up into the air, and fell of all places in the world into Lady Mary's lap.

Mr Fox looked about a bit, but did not think of looking behind the cask, so at last he went on dragging the young lady up the stairs into the Bloody Chamber.

As soon as she heard him pass through the gallery, Lady Mary crept out of the door, down through the gateway, and ran home as fast as she could.

Now it happened that the very next day the marriage contract of Lady Mary and Mr Fox was to be signed, and there was a splendid breakfast before that. And when Mr Fox was seated at table opposite Lady Mary, he looked at her. 'How pale you are this morning, my dear.' 'Yes,' said she, 'I had a bad night's rest last night. I had horrible dreams.' 'Dreams go by contraries,' said Mr Fox; 'but tell us your dream, and your sweet voice will make the time pass till the happy hour comes.'

'I dreamed,' said Lady Mary, 'that I went yestermorn to your castle, and I found it in the woods, with high walls, and a deep moat, and over the gateway was written:

> Be bold, be bold.'

'But it is not so, nor it was not so,' said Mr Fox.
'And when I came to the doorway, over it was written:

> Be bold, be bold, but not too bold.'

'It is not so, nor it was not so,' said Mr Fox.
'And then I went upstairs, and came to a gallery, at the end of which was a door, on which was written:

> Be bold, be bold, but not too bold,
> Lest that your heart's blood should run cold.'

'It is not so, nor it was not so,' said Mr Fox.
'And then – and then I opened the door, and the room was filled with bodies and skeletons of poor dead women, all stained with their blood.'

'It is not so, nor it was not so. And God forbid it should be so,' said Mr Fox.

'I then dreamed that I rushed down the gallery, and just as I was going down the stairs I saw you, Mr Fox, coming up to the hall door, dragging after you a poor young lady, rich and beautiful.'

'It is not so, nor it was not so. And God forbid it should be so,' said Mr Fox.

'I rushed downstairs, just in time to hide myself behind a cask, when you, Mr Fox, came in dragging the young lady by the arm. And, as you passed me, Mr Fox, I thought I saw you try and get off her diamond ring, and when you could not, Mr Fox, it seemed to me in my dream, that you out with your sword and hacked off the poor lady's hand to get the ring.'

'It is not so, nor it was not so. And God forbid it should be so,' said Mr Fox, and was going to say something else as he rose from his seat, when Lady Mary cried out:

'But it is so, and it was so. Here's hand and ring I have to show', and pulled out the lady's hand from her dress, and pointed it straight at Mr Fox.

At once her brothers and her friends drew their swords and cut Mr Fox into a thousand pieces.

The Old Woman and her Pig

*

AN OLD WOMAN was sweeping her house, and she found a little crooked sixpence. 'What,' said she, 'shall I do with this little sixpence? I will go to market, and buy a little pig.'

As she was coming home, she came to a stile: but the piggy wouldn't go over the stile.

She went a little further, and she met a dog. So she said to him: 'Dog! dog! bite pig; piggy won't go over the stile; and I shan't get home tonight.' But the dog wouldn't.

She went a little further, and met a stick. So she said: 'Stick! stick! beat dog! dog won't bite pig; piggy won't get over the stile; and I shan't get home tonight.' But the stick wouldn't.

She went a little further, and she met a fire. So she said: 'Fire! fire! burn stick; stick won't beat dog; dog won't bite pig; piggy won't get over the stile; and I shan't get home tonight.' But the fire wouldn't.

She went a little further, and she met some water. So she said: 'Water! water! quench fire; fire won't burn stick; stick won't beat dog; dog won't bite pig; piggy won't get over the stile; and I shan't get home tonight.' But the water wouldn't.

She went a little further, and she met an ox. So she said: 'Ox! ox! drink water; water won't quench fire; fire won't burn stick; stick won't beat dog; dog won't bite pig; piggy won't get over the stile; and I shan't get home tonight.' But the ox wouldn't.

She went a little further, and she met a butcher. So she said: 'Butcher! butcher! kill ox; ox won't drink water; water won't quench fire; fire won't burn stick; stick won't beat dog; dog won't bite pig; piggy won't get over the stile; and I shan't get home tonight.' But the butcher wouldn't.

She went a little further, and she met a rope. So she said: 'Rope! rope! hang butcher; butcher won't kill ox; ox won't drink water; water won't quench fire; fire won't burn stick; stick won't beat dog; dog won't bite pig; piggy won't get over the stile; and I shan't get home tonight.' But the rope wouldn't.

She went a little further, and she met a rat. So she said: 'Rat! rat! gnaw rope; rope won't hang butcher; butcher won't kill ox; ox won't drink water; water won't quench fire; fire won't burn stick; stick won't beat dog; dog won't bite pig; piggy won't get over the stile; and I shan't get home tonight.' But the rat wouldn't.

She went a little further, and she met a cat. So she said: 'Cat! cat! kill rat; rat won't gnaw rope; rope won't hang butcher; butcher won't kill ox; ox won't drink water; water won't quench fire; fire won't burn stick; stick won't beat dog; dog won't bite pig; piggy won't get over the stile; and I shan't get home tonight.' But the cat said to her, 'If you will go to yonder cow, and fetch me a saucer of milk, I will kill the rat.' So away went the old woman to the cow.

But the cow said to her: 'If you will go to yonder hay-stack, and fetch me a handful of hay, I'll give you the milk.' So away went the old woman to the hay-stack; and she brought the hay to the cow.

As soon as the cow had eaten the hay, she gave the old woman the milk; and away she went with it in a saucer to the cat.

As soon as the cat lapped up the milk, the cat began to kill the rat; the rat began to gnaw the rope; the rope began to hang the butcher; the butcher began to kill the ox; the ox began to drink the water; the water began to quench the fire; the fire began to burn the stick; the stick began to beat the dog; the dog began to bite the pig; the little pig in a fright jumped over the stile; and so the old woman got home that night.

The History of Tom Thumb

*

IN THE DAYS of the great Prince Arthur there lived a mighty
magician, called Merlin, the most learned and skilful enchanter
the world has ever seen.

This famous magician, who could take any form he pleased,
was travelling about as a poor beggar, and being very tired he
stopped at the cottage of a ploughman to rest himself, and
asked for some food.

The countryman bade him welcome, and his wife, who was a
very good-hearted woman, soon brought him some milk in a
wooden bowl, and some coarse brown bread on a platter.

Merlin was much pleased with the kindness of the plough-
man and his wife; but he could not help noticing that though

everything was neat and comfortable in the cottage they both seemed to be very unhappy. He therefore asked them why they were so melancholy, and learned that they were miserable because they had no children.

The poor woman said, with tears in her eyes: 'I should be the happiest creature in the world if I had a son; although he was no bigger than my husband's thumb, I would be satisfied.'

Merlin was so much amused with the idea of a boy no bigger than a man's thumb that he determined to grant the poor woman's wish. Accordingly, in a short time after, the plough-man's wife had a son, who, wonderful to relate! was not a bit bigger than his father's thumb.

The queen of the fairies, wishing to see the little fellow, came in at the window while the mother was sitting up in the bed admiring him. The queen kissed the child, and, giving it the name of Tom Thumb, sent for some of the fairies, who dressed her little godson according to her orders:

> An oak-leaf hat he had for his crown;
> His shirt of web by spiders spun;
> With jacket wove of thistle's down;
> His trousers were of feathers done.
> His stockings, of apple-rind, they tie
> With eyelash from his mother's eye:
> His shoes were made of mouse's skin,
> Tann'd with the downy hair within.

Tom never grew any larger than his father's thumb, which was only of ordinary size; but as he got older he became very cunning and full of tricks. When he was old enough to play with the boys, and had lost all his own cherry-stones, he used to creep into the bags of his playfellows, fill his pockets, and, getting out without their noticing him, would again join in the game.

One day, however, as he was coming out of a bag of cherry-stones, where he had been stealing as usual, the boy to whom it belonged chanced to see him. 'Ah, ah! my little Tommy,' said the boy, 'so I have caught you stealing my cherry-stones at last, and you shall be rewarded for your thievish tricks.' On saying this, he drew the string tight round his neck, and gave the bag such a hearty shake that poor little Tom's legs, thighs, and body were sadly bruised. He roared out with pain, and begged to be let out, promising never to steal again.

A short time afterwards his mother was making a batter-pudding, and Tom, being very anxious to see how it was made, climbed up to the edge of the bowl; but his foot slipped, and he plumped over head and ears into the batter, without his mother noticing him, who stirred him into the pudding-bag, and put him in the pot to boil.

The batter filled Tom's mouth, and prevented him from crying; but, on feeling the hot water, he kicked and struggled so much in the pot that his mother thought that the pudding was bewitched, and, pulling it out of the pot, she threw it outside the door. A poor tinker, who was passing by, lifted up the pudding, and, putting it into his budget, he then walked off. As Tom had now got his mouth cleared of the batter, he then began to cry aloud, which so frightened the tinker that he flung down the pudding and ran away. The pudding being broke to pieces by the fall, Tom crept out covered all over with the batter, and walked home. His mother, who was very sorry to see her darling in such a woeful state, put him into a teacup, and soon washed off the batter; after which she kissed him, and laid him in bed.

Soon after the adventure of the pudding, Tom's mother went to milk her cow in the meadow, and she took him along with her. As the wind was very high, for fear of being blown away, she tied him to a thistle with a piece of fine thread. The cow soon observed Tom's oak-leaf hat, and liking the appearance of it, took poor Tom and the thistle at one mouthful. While the cow was chewing the thistle, Tom was afraid of her great teeth, which threatened to crush him in pieces, and he roared out as loud as he could: 'Mother, mother!'

'Where are you, Tommy, my dear Tommy?' said his mother.

'Here, mother,' replied he, 'in the red cow's mouth.'

His mother began to cry and wring her hands; but the cow,

surprised at the odd noise in her throat, opened her mouth and let Tom drop out. Fortunately his mother caught him in her apron as he was falling to the ground, or he would have been dreadfully hurt. She then put Tom in her bosom and ran home with him.

Tom's father made him a whip of a barley straw to drive the cattle with, and having one day gone into the fields, Tom slipped a foot and rolled into the furrow. A raven, which was flying over, picked him up, and flew with him over the sea, and there dropped him.

A large fish swallowed Tom the moment he fell into the sea, which was soon after caught, and bought for the table of King Arthur. When they opened the fish in order to cook it, everyone was astonished at finding such a little boy, and Tom was quite delighted at being free again. They carried him to the king, who made Tom his dwarf, and he soon grew a great favourite at court; for by his tricks and gambols he not only amused the king and queen, but also all the Knights of the Round Table.

It is said that when the king rode out on horseback, he often took Tom along with him, and if a shower came on, he used to creep into his majesty's waistcoat pocket, where he slept till the rain was over.

King Arthur one day asked Tom about his parents, wishing to know if they were as small as he was, and whether they were well off. Tom told the king that his father and mother were as tall as anybody about the court, but in rather poor circumstances. On hearing this, the king carried Tom to the treasury, the place where he kept all his money, and told him to take as much money as he could carry home to his parents, which made the poor little fellow caper with joy. Tom went immediately to procure a purse, which was made of a water-bubble, and then returned to the treasury, where he received a silver three-penny-piece to put into it.

Our little hero had some difficulty in lifting the burden upon his back; but he at last succeeded in getting it placed to his mind, and set forward on his journey. However, without meeting with any accident, and after resting himself more than a hundred times by the way, in two days and two nights he reached his father's house in safety.

Tom had travelled forty-eight hours with a huge silver-piece on his back, and was almost tired to death, when his mother ran out to meet him, and carried him into the house. But he soon returned to court.

As Tom's clothes had suffered much in the batter-pudding, and the inside of the fish, his majesty ordered him a new suit of clothes, and to be mounted as a knight on a mouse.

Of Butterfly's wings his shirt was made,
   His boots of chicken's hide;
And by a nimble fairy blade,
Well learned in the tailoring trade,
   His clothing was supplied.
   A needle dangled by his side;
   A dapper mouse he used to ride,
   Thus strutted Tom in stately pride!

It was certainly very diverting to see Tom in this dress and mounted on the mouse, as he rode out a-hunting with the king and nobility, who were all ready to expire with laughter at Tom and his fine prancing charger.

The king was so charmed with his address that he ordered a little chair to be made, in order that Tom might sit upon his table, and also a palace of gold, a span high, with a door an inch wide, to live in. He also gave him a coach, drawn by six small mice.

The queen was so enraged at the honours conferred on Sir Thomas that she resolved to ruin him, and told the king that the little knight had been saucy to her.

The king sent for Tom in great haste, but being fully aware of the danger of royal anger, he crept into an empty snail-shell, where he lay for a long time until he was almost starved with hunger; but at last he ventured to peep out, and seeing a fine large butterfly on the ground, near the place of his concealment, he got close to it and jumping astride on it, was carried up into the air. The butterfly flew with him from tree to tree and from field to field, and at last returned to the court, where the king and nobility all strove to catch him; but at last poor Tom fell from his seat into a watering-pot, in which he was almost drowned.

When the queen saw him, she was in a rage, and said he should be beheaded; and he was again put into a mouse trap until the time of his execution.

However, a cat, observing something alive in the trap, patted it about till the wires broke, and set Thomas at liberty.

The king received Tom again into favour, which he did not live to enjoy, for a large spider one day attacked him; and although he drew his sword and fought well, yet the spider's poisonous breath at last overcame him.

> He fell dead on the ground where he stood,
> And the spider suck'd every drop of his blood.

King Arthur and his whole court were so sorry at the loss of

their little favourite that they went into mourning and raised a
fine white marble monument over his grave with the following
epitaph:

> Here lies Tom Thumb, King Arthur's knight,
> Who died by a spider's cruel bite.
> He was well known in Arthur's court,
> Where he afforded gallant sport;
> He rode a tilt and tournament,
> And on a mouse a-hunting went.
> Alive he filled the court with mirth;
> His death to sorrow soon gave birth.
> Wipe, wipe your eyes, and shake your head
> And cry, – Alas! Tom Thumb is dead!

The Three Sillies

*

ONCE UPON A TIME there was a farmer and his wife who had
one daughter, and she was courted by a gentleman. Every
evening he used to come and see her, and stop to supper at the
farmhouse, and the daughter used to be sent down into the
cellar to draw the beer for supper. So one evening she had gone
down to draw the beer, and she happened to look up at the
ceiling while she was drawing, and she saw a mallet stuck in
one of the beams. It must have been there a long, long time,
but somehow or other she had never noticed it before, and she
began a-thinking. And she thought it was very dangerous to
have that mallet there, for she said to herself: 'Suppose him
and me was to be married, and we was to have a son, and he
was to grow up to be a man, and come down into the cellar to
draw the beer, like as I'm doing now, and the mallet was to
fall on his head and kill him, what a dreadful thing it would be!'

And she put down the candle and the jug, and sat herself down and began a-crying.

Well, they began to wonder upstairs how it was that she was so long drawing the beer, and her mother went down to see after her, and she found her sitting on the settle crying, and the beer running over the floor. 'Why, whatever is the matter?' said her mother. 'Oh, mother!' says she, 'look at that horrid mallet! Suppose we was to be married, and was to have a son, and he was to grow up, and was to come down to the cellar to draw the beer, and the mallet was to fall on his head and kill him, what a dreadful thing it would be!' 'Dear, dear! what a dreadful thing it would be!' said the mother, and she sat her down aside of the daughter and started a-crying too. Then after a bit the father began to wonder that they didn't come back, and he went down into the cellar to look after them himself, and there they two sat a-crying, and the beer running all over the floor. 'Whatever is the matter?' says he. 'Why,' says the mother, 'look at that horrid mallet. Just suppose, if our daughter and her sweetheart was to be married, and was to have a son, and he was to grow up, and was to come down into the cellar to draw the beer, and the mallet was to fall on his head and kill him, what a dreadful thing it would be!' 'Dear, dear, dear! so it would!' said the father, and he sat himself down aside of the other two, and started a-crying.

Now the gentleman got tired of stopping up in the kitchen by himself, and at last went down into the cellar, too, to see what they were after; and there they three sat a-crying side by side, and the beer running all over the floor. And he ran straight and turned the tap. Then he said: 'Whatever are you three doing, sitting there crying, and letting the beer run all over the floor?' 'Oh!' says the father, 'look at that horrid mallet! Suppose you and our daughter was to be married, and was to have a son, and he was to grow up, and was to come down into the cellar to draw the beer, and the mallet was to fall on his head and kill him!' And then they all started a-crying worse than before. But the gentleman burst out a-laughing, and reached up and pulled out the mallet, and then he said: 'I've travelled many miles, and I never met three such big sillies as you three before; and now I shall start out on my travels again, and when I can find three bigger sillies than you three, then I'll come back and marry your daughter.' So he wished them good-bye, and started off on his travels, and left them all crying because the girl had lost her sweetheart.

Well, he set out, and he travelled a long way, and at last he came to a woman's cottage that had some grass growing on the roof. And the woman was trying to get her cow to go up a ladder to the grass, and the poor thing durst not go. So the gentleman asked the woman what she was doing. 'Why, lookye,' she said, 'look at all the beautiful grass. I'm going to get the cow on to the roof to eat it. She'll be quite safe, for I shall tie a string round her neck, and pass it down the chimney, and tie it to my wrist as I go about the house, so she can't fall off without my knowing it.' 'Oh, you poor silly!' said the gentleman, 'you should cut the grass and throw it down to the

cow!' But the woman thought it was easier to get the cow up
the ladder than to get the grass down, so she pushed her and
coaxed her and got her up, and tied a string round her neck,
and passed it down the chimney, and fastened it to her own
wrist. And the gentleman went on his way, but he hadn't
gone far when the cow tumbled off the roof, and hung by the
string tied round her neck, and it strangled her. And the weight
of the cow tied to her wrist pulled the woman up the chimney,
and she stuck fast half-way and was smothered in the soot.

Well, that was one big silly.

And the gentleman went on and on, and he went to an inn
to stop the night, and they were so full at the inn that they had
to put him in a double-bedded room, and another tráveller was
to sleep in the other bed. The other man was a very pleasant
fellow, and they got very friendly together; but in the morning,
when they were both getting up, the gentleman was surprised
to see the other hang his trousers on the knobs of the chest of
drawers and run across the room and try to jump into them,
and he tried over and over again and couldn't manage it; and
the gentleman wondered whatever he was doing it for. At last
he stopped and wiped his face with his handkerchief. 'Oh dear,'
he says, 'I do think trousers are the most awkwardest kind of
clothes that ever were. I can't think who could have invented
such things. It takes me the best part of an hour to get into
mine every morning, and I get so hot! How do you manage
yours?' So the gentleman burst out a-laughing, and showed
him how to put them on; and he was very much obliged to him,
and said he never should have thought of doing it that way.

So that was another big silly.

Then the gentleman went on his travels again; and he came
to a village, and outside the village there was a pond, and round
the pond was a crowd of people. And they had got rakes, and
brooms, and pitchforks reaching into the pond; and the gentleman asked what was the matter. 'Why,' they say, 'matter
enough! Moon's tumbled into the pond and we can't rake her
out anyhow!' So the gentleman burst out a-laughing, and told
them to look up into the sky, and that it was only the shadow

in the water. But they wouldn't listen to him, and abused him shamefully, and he got away as quick as he could.

So there was a whole lot of sillies bigger than them three sillies at home. So the gentleman turned back home again and married the farmer's daughter, and if they didn't live happy for ever after, that's nothing to do with you or me.

Mr Vinegar

*

MR AND MRS VINEGAR lived in a vinegar bottle. Now, one
day, when Mr Vinegar was from home, Mrs Vinegar, who
was a very good housewife, was busily sweeping her house,
when an unlucky thump of the broom brought the whole house
clitter-clatter, clitter-clatter, about her ears. In an agony of
grief she rushed forth to meet her husband. On seeing him she
exclaimed, 'O Mr Vinegar, Mr Vinegar, we are ruined, we are
ruined: I have knocked the house down, and it is all to pieces!'
Mr Vinegar then said: 'My dear, let us see what can be done.
Here is the door; I will take it on my back, and we will go
forth to seek our fortune.' They walked all that day, and at
nightfall entered a thick forest. They were both very, very
tired, and Mr Vinegar said: 'My love, I will climb up into a
tree, drag up the door, and you shall follow.' He accordingly
did so, and they both stretched their weary limbs on the door,
and fell fast asleep. In the middle of the night, Mr Vinegar was
disturbed by the sound of voices underneath, and to his horror
and dismay found that it was a band of thieves met to divide
their booty. 'Here, Jack,' said one, 'there's five pounds for you;
here, Bill, here's ten pounds for you; here, Bob, there's three
pounds for you.' Mr Vinegar could listen no longer; his terror
was so great that he trembled and trembled, and shook down
the door on their heads. Away scampered the thieves, but Mr
Vinegar dared not quit his retreat till broad daylight. He
then scrambled out of the tree, and went to lift up the door.
What did he see but a number of golden guineas. 'Come down,
Mrs Vinegar,' he cried; 'come down, I say; our fortune's made,
our fortune's made! Come down, I say.' Mrs Vinegar got down
as fast as she could, and when she saw the money, she jumped
for joy. 'Now, my dear,' said she, 'I'll tell you what you shall do.
There is a fair at the neighbouring town; you shall take these

forty guineas and buy a cow. I can make butter and cheese, which you shall sell at market, and we shall then be able to live very comfortably.' Mr Vinegar joyfully agrees, takes the money, and off he goes to the fair. When he arrived, he walked up and down, and at length saw a beautiful red cow. It was an excellent milker, and perfect in every way. 'Oh!' thought Mr Vinegar, 'if I had but that cow, I should be the happiest man alive.' So he offered the forty guineas for the cow, and the owner said that,

as he was a friend, he'd oblige him. So the bargain was made, and he got the cow and he drove it backwards and forwards to show it. By and by he saw a man playing the bagpipes – Tweedle-dum, tweedle-dee. The children followed him about, and he appeared to be pocketing money on all sides. 'Well,' thought Mr Vinegar, 'if I had but that beautiful instrument I should be the happiest man alive – my fortune would be made.' So he went up to the man. 'Friend,' says he, 'what a beautiful instru-ment that is, and what a deal of money you must make.' 'Why, yes,' said the man, 'I make a great deal of money, to be sure, and it is a wonderful instrument.' 'Oh!' cried Mr Vinegar, 'how I should like to possess it!' 'Well,' said the man, 'as you are a friend, I don't much mind parting with it: you shall have it for that red cow.' 'Done!' said the delighted Mr Vinegar. So the beautiful red cow was given for the bagpipes. He walked up and down with his purchase; but it was in vain he tried to play a tune, and instead of pocketing pence, the boys followed him hooting, laughing, and pelting.

Poor Mr Vinegar, his fingers grew very cold, and, just as he was leaving the town, he met a man with a fine thick pair of gloves. 'Oh, my fingers are so very cold,' said Mr Vinegar to himself. 'Now if I had but those beautiful gloves I should be the happiest man alive.' He went up to the man, and said to him: 'Friend, you seem to have a capital pair of gloves there.' 'Yes, truly,' cried the man; 'and my hands are as warm as possible this cold November day.' 'Well,' said Mr Vinegar, 'I should like to have them.' 'What will you give?' said the man; 'as you are a friend, I don't much mind letting you have them for those bagpipes.' 'Done!' cried Mr Vinegar. He put on the gloves, and felt perfectly happy as he trudged homewards.

At last he grew very tired, when he saw a man coming towards him with a good stout stick in his hand.

'Oh,' said Mr Vinegar, 'that I had but that stick! I should then be the happiest man alive.' He said to the man: 'Friend, what a rare good stick you have got!' 'Yes,' said the man; 'I have used it for many a long mile, and a good friend it has been; but if you have a fancy for it, as you are a friend, I don't mind giving it to you for that pair of gloves.' Mr Vinegar's hands were so warm, and his legs so tired, that he gladly made the exchange. As he drew near to the wood where he had left his wife, he heard a parrot on a tree calling out his name: 'Mr Vinegar, you foolish man, you blockhead, you simpleton; you went to the fair, and laid out all your money in buying a cow. Not content with that, you changed it for bagpipes, on which you could not play, and which were not worth one-tenth of the money. You fool, you – you had no sooner got the bagpipes than you changed them for the gloves, which were not worth one-quarter of the money; and when you had got the gloves, you changed them for a poor miserable stick; and now for your forty guineas, cow, bagpipes, and gloves, you have nothing to show but that poor miserable stick, which you might have cut in any hedge.' On this the bird laughed and laughed, and Mr Vinegar, falling into a violent rage, threw the stick at its head. The stick lodged in the tree, and he returned to his wife without money, cow, bagpipes, gloves, or stick, and she instantly gave him such a sound cudgelling that she almost broke every bone in his skin.

The Story of the Three Bears

*

ONCE UPON A TIME there were Three Bears, who lived together in a house of their own, in a wood. One of them was a Little, Small, Wee Bear; and one was a Middle-sized Bear, and the other was a Great, Huge Bear. They had each a pot for their porridge, a little pot for the Little, Small, Wee Bear, and a middle-sized pot for the Middle Bear, and a great pot for the Great, Huge Bear. And they each had a chair to sit in; a little chair for the Little, Small, Wee Bear; and a middle-sized chair for the Middle Bear; and a great chair for the Great, Huge Bear. And they each had a bed to sleep in; a little bed for the Little, Small, Wee Bear; and a middle-sized bed for the Middle Bear; and a great bed for the Great, Huge Bear.

One day, after they had made the porridge for their breakfast, and poured it into their porridge-pots, they walked out into the wood while the porridge was cooling, that they might not burn their mouths, by beginning too soon to eat it. And while they were walking, a little old Woman came to the house. She could not have been a good, honest old Woman; for first she looked in at the window, and then she peeped in at the keyhole; and seeing nobody in the house, she lifted the latch. The door was not fastened, because the Bears were good Bears, who did nobody any harm, and never suspected that anybody would harm them. So the little old Woman opened the door, and went in; and well pleased she was when she saw the porridge on the table. If she had been a good little old Woman, she would have waited till the Bears came home, and then, perhaps, they would have asked her to breakfast; for they were good Bears – a little rough or so, as the manner of Bears is, but for all that very good-natured and hospitable. But she was an impudent, bad old Woman, and set about helping herself.

So first she tasted the porridge of the Great, Huge Bear, and that was too hot for her; and she said a bad word about that. And then she tasted the porridge of the Middle Bear, and that was too cold for her; and she said a bad word about that, too. And then she went to the porridge of the Little, Small, Wee Bear, and tasted that; and that was neither too hot nor too cold, but just right; and she liked it so well that she ate it all up: but the naughty old Woman said a bad word about the little porridge-pot, because it did not hold enough for her.

Then the little old Woman sate down in the chair of the Great, Huge Bear, and that was too hard for her. And then she sate down in the chair of the Middle Bear, and that was too soft for her. And then she sate down in the chair of the Little, Small, Wee Bear, and that was neither too hard, nor too soft, but just right. So she seated herself in it, and there she sate till the bottom of the chair came out, and down she came, plump upon the ground. And the naughty old Woman said a wicked word about that, too.

Then the little old Woman went upstairs into the bed-chamber in which the three Bears slept. And first she lay down upon the bed of the Great, Huge Bear; but that was too high at the head for her. And next she lay down upon the bed of the Middle Bear, and that was too high at the foot for her. And then she lay down upon the bed of the Little, Small, Wee Bear, and that was neither too high at the head nor at the foot, but just right. So she covered herself up comfortably, and lay there till she fell fast asleep.

By this time the Three Bears thought their porridge would be cool enough, so they came home to breakfast. Now the little old Woman had left the spoon of the Great, Huge Bear, standing in his porridge.

'Somebody has been at my porridge!'

said the Great, Huge Bear, in his great, rough, gruff voice. And when the Middle Bear looked at his, he saw that the spoon was standing in it, too. They were wooden spoons; if they had been silver ones, the naughty old Woman would have put them in her pocket.

'Somebody has been at my porridge!'

said the Middle Bear in his middle voice.

Then the Little, Small, Wee Bear looked at his, and there was the spoon in the porridge-pot, but the porridge was all gone.

'Somebody has been at my porridge, and has eaten it all up!'

said the Little, Small, Wee Bear, in his little, small, wee voice.

Upon this the Three Bears, seeing that someone had entered their house, and eaten up the Little, Small, Wee Bear's breakfast, began to look about them. Now the little old Woman had not put the hard cushion straight when she rose from the chair of the Great, Huge Bear.

'Somebody has been sitting in my chair!'

said the Great, Huge Bear, in his great, rough, gruff voice.

And the little old Woman had squatted down the soft cushion of the Middle Bear.

'Somebody has been sitting in my chair!'

said the Middle Bear, in his middle voice.

And you know what the little old Woman had done to the third chair.

'Somebody has been sitting in my chair and has sate the bottom out of it!'

said the Little, Small, Wee Bear, in his little, small, wee voice.

Then the three Bears thought it necessary that they should make further search; so they went upstairs into their bed-chamber. Now the little old Woman had pulled the pillow of the Great, Huge Bear out of its place.

'Somebody has been lying in my bed!'

said the Great, Huge Bear, in his great, rough, gruff voice.

And the little old Woman had pulled the bolster of the Middle Bear out of its place.

'Somebody has been lying in my bed!'

said the Middle Bear, in his middle voice.

And when the Little, Small, Wee Bear came to look at his bed, there was the bolster in its right place, and the pillow in its place upon the bolster; and upon the pillow was the little old Woman's ugly, dirty head – which was not in its place, for she had no business there.

'Somebody has been lying in my bed—and here she is!'

said the Little, Small, Wee Bear, in his little, small, wee voice.

The little old Woman had heard in her sleep the great, rough, gruff voice of the Great, Huge Bear; but she was so fast asleep that it was no more to her than the roaring of wind or the rumbling of thunder. And she had heard the middle voice, of the Middle Bear, but it was only as if she had heard someone speaking in a dream. But when she heard the little, small, wee voice of the Little, Small, Wee Bear, it was so sharp, and so shrill, that it awakened her at once. Up she started; and when she saw the Three Bears on one side of the bed, she tumbled herself out at the other, and ran to the window. Now the window was open, because the Bears, like good, tidy Bears as they were, always opened their bed-chamber window when they got up in the morning. Out the little old Woman jumped; and whether she broke her neck in the fall; or ran into the wood and was lost there; or found her way out of the wood, and was taken up by the constable and sent to the House of Correction for a vagrant as she was, I cannot tell. But the Three Bears never saw anything more of her.